FIRST AMERICAN EDITION

First published in Great Britain by
Walker Books Ltd., London

Library of Congress Catalog Card Number 86-82088
ISBN 0-87113-127-7

PRINTED IN ITALY

Good Night, Little Rabbit

Marie Wabbes

The Atlantic Monthly Press
Boston   New York

Little Rabbit takes his bath.

He wraps himself
in his big, blue bath towel.

He puts on his pajamas.
He eats a carrot for a treat.

He sits on his potty.

Then, he brushes his teeth.

Quick, hop into bed.
What's the matter, Little Rabbit?

Where is Woolly Rabbit?

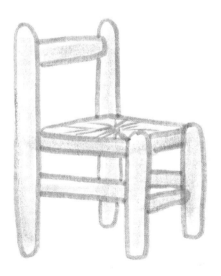

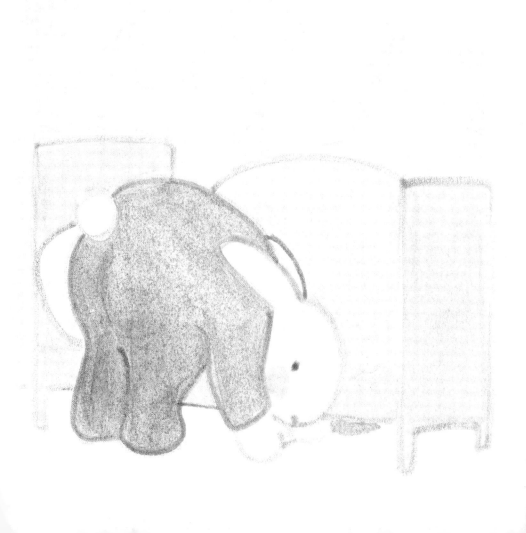

Come to bed, Woolly Rabbit.

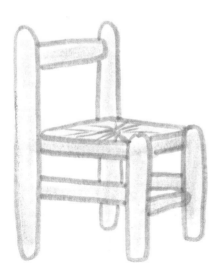

Good night, Little Rabbit.
Good night, Woolly Rabbit.
Sleep tight.